GAYLORD

AUTHOR'S DAY

written and illustrated by
DANIEL PINKWATER

Macmillan Publishing Company   New York   Maxwell Macmillan Canada   Toronto
Maxwell Macmillan International   New York   Oxford   Singapore   Sydney

First edition

Printed in the United States of America

10 9 8 7 6 5 4 3 2 1

The text of this book is set in 14 pt. Egyptian 505.
The illustrations are rendered in pen and ink with color markers.

Library of Congress Cataloging-in-Publication Data
Pinkwater, Daniel Manus, date. Author's day / written and illustrated by Daniel Pinkwater. – 1st ed.   p.   cm.
Summary: In this comedy of errors, a famous children's author visits an elementary school. ISBN 0-02-774642-9 [1. Authors — Fiction. 2. Authorship – Fiction. 3. Schools – Fiction. 4. Humorous stories.] I. Title. PZ7.P6335Aw 1993
[E] – dc20   92-18154

To Jill, who knows how to treat an author

I t was Author's Day at Melvinville Elementary School.

Mr. Carramba, the librarian, arrived early. He made sure the school library was tidy. He made sure there was no chewing gum in the water fountains. He dragged a ladder to the front door of the school. He climbed up the ladder and hung a big banner over the door. It said:

WELCOME MR. BRAMWELL WINK-PORTER

AUTHOR OF THE FUZZY BUNNY

The next person to arrive was the principal, Mrs. Feenbogen. "Is everything ready?" Mrs. Feenbogen asked Mr. Carramba.

"I think so," Mr. Carramba said.

Howard the janitor arrived. "Who used my ladder?" Howard asked.

The teachers arrived. The buses arrived. The children got out of the buses. They looked up at the banner. "Is Bramwell Wink-Porter here yet?" the children asked.

The teachers and children went to their classrooms. Mr. Carramba was in the library. Mrs. Feenbogen was in the office. Howard the janitor carried his ladder to the basement. In the lunchroom, the lunchroom people were making lunch. Everybody was excited, waiting.

A rusty green car came into the parking lot. Driving the car was a man drinking coffee out of a plastic foam cup. Empty plastic foam cups rattled and rolled on the floor of the car. The car had a noisy motor, and made a lot of smoke. It had a bumper sticker that said: **I'D RATHER BE WRITING.**

The car came to a stop, and Bramwell Wink-Porter, the famous author, got out. He looked up at the banner over the door of the school. "I did not write *The Fuzzy Bunny*," Bramwell Wink-Porter said to himself. "The name of my book is *The Bunny Brothers*."

Mr. Carramba and Mrs. Feenbogen came out of the school. "Welcome to Melvinville Elementary School," Mrs. Feenbogen said.

"All the children are excited," Mr. Carramba said. "They have all read your book, *The Fuzzy Bunny*."

"I did not write *The Fuzzy Bunny*," Bramwell Wink-Porter said.

"Such modesty!" Mrs. Feenbogen said.

"*The Fuzzy Bunny* was written by Abigail Finkdotter," Bramwell Wink-Porter said. "Not me."

"I have never met a famous author," said Mr. Carramba. "This is the most exciting thing that has ever happened to me."

"My book is called *The Bunny Brothers*," Bramwell Wink-Porter said.

"I am so thrilled that you are here," said Mr. Carramba.

"Yes," said Mrs. Feenbogen. "So am I. And perhaps you could talk about *The Fuzzy Bunny*, even though you did not write it."

"Come to the library," Mr. Carramba said. "We have just gotten a box of your books. This is so exciting!"

In the library, Mr. Carramba opened a large box. "This just came," he said. "Here are many copies of your book."

"This book is *Bunnies for Breakfast* by Lemuel Crankstarter," Bramwell Wink-Porter said. "I did not write this. My book is called *The Bunny Brothers.*"

"Well, it is time to get started," Mr. Carramba said. "You will begin with a visit to the kindergarten class. But first...I am so excited...I think I am going to faint."

Mr. Carramba threw himself to the floor.

"Oh! Mr. Carramba has fainted!" Mrs. Feenbogen said. "Send for Howard the janitor!"

"Wouldn't it be better to send for the nurse?" Bramwell Wink-Porter asked.

"Howard is also a nurse," Mrs. Feenbogen said. "He will take care of Mr. Carramba."

Mrs. Feenbogen stepped over Mr. Carramba, and took Bramwell Wink-Porter to the kindergarten. "The kindergarten teacher's name is Mrs. Neatfeet," she told him.

The kindergarten class had made pancakes for a treat. The pancakes were lumpy and dirty. Some of the pancakes had pieces of crayon in them. The children were having fun playing with syrup.

"Look, class!" Mrs. Neatfeet said. "It is Mr. Bramwell Wink-Porter, author of *The Fuzzy Bunny*!"

"*The Bunny Brothers*," Bramwell Wink-Porter said.

"Shall we give Mr. Bramwell Wink-Porter a hug?" Mrs. Neatfeet asked the kindergarten class.

The kindergartners crowded around Bramwell Wink-Porter, and hugged him.

"They are very sticky children," Bramwell Wink-Porter said.

"They are not usually this sticky," Mrs. Neatfeet told him. "It is the syrup."

"Yes," said Bramwell Wink-Porter.

After being made to eat a cold, lumpy pancake with a piece of green crayon in it, Bramwell Wink-Porter was taken to meet the first graders.

"Don't come in yet!" said Mrs. Fleetstreet, the first grade teacher. "We have a surprise for you."

The surprise was that all the first graders had Fuzzy Bunny masks, and Fuzzy Bunny hats with ears. They had made the masks and hats themselves.

"What a surprise," said Bramwell Wink-Porter.

"We love *The Fuzzy Bunny*!" the first graders all said at the same time.

"Thank you," said Bramwell Wink-Porter.

Wearing the adult-size Fuzzy Bunny hat with ears the first grade had given him, Bramwell Wink-Porter was taken to the gym to talk with the second and third grades.

The second and third graders had prepared questions to ask the famous author.

"Was it hard to write *The Fuzzy Bunny*?" they asked him.

"No, it was not very hard...I suppose," Bramwell Wink-Porter said.

"What is your favorite book?" another child asked.

"My favorite book is *Moby Dick* by Herman Melville," Bramwell Wink-Porter answered.

"No – I mean your favorite book that you wrote."

"Oh. Well, I'd have to say *The Bunny Brothers*," Bramwell Wink-Porter said.

The second and third graders looked at one another.

"You haven't read that one, have you?" Bramwell Wink-Porter said. "Well, I hope you will."

"What is your favorite rodent?"

"That's easy – a bunny," said Bramwell Wink-Porter.

"A bunny isn't properly a rodent. Bunnies belong to the order Lagomorpha."

"In that case, I'd say gerbils are my favorite rodents. Gerbils are rodents, aren't they?"

"What is your favorite ladies' shoe?"

"A light green high-heeled sandal, size eight."

"What is your own shoe size?"

"Ten."

"Do you have a favorite kind of toast?"

"Yes, raisin."

"What is the greatest number of hot dogs you have eaten at one sitting?"

"Eleven."

"Have you ever been to South America?"

"No."

"Would you like to go there?"

"Yes."

"Which is better, grape soda or ginger ale?"

"Grape soda."

"Have you ever been bitten by a horse?"

"Yes."

"That's all the time we have, children," Mrs. Feenbogen said. "Let's give Mr. Bramwell Wink-Porter a big hand."

The second and third grades applauded, and Mrs. Feenbogen led Bramwell Wink-Porter out of the gym.

"How is Mr. Carramba?" Bramwell Wink-Porter asked.

"He is fine," Mrs. Feenbogen said. "Howard the janitor says he just got too excited. Now it is time to eat lunch with the teachers."

Mrs. Feenbogen took Bramwell Wink-Porter to the teachers' lunchroom. There was Mr. Carramba. He was holding a damp paper towel to his forehead.

"I am much better," Mr. Carramba said. "It is just that having you, a famous author, visit our school is just so wonderful!" Mr. Carramba got to his feet.

"Careful!" Howard the janitor said. "You'll faint again!"

"I do feel a little dizzy," Mr. Carramba said. "I'll just lie down on the table."

Mr. Carramba stretched out on the table, and held the damp paper towel to his forehead. Some teachers brought sandwiches, and carefully put them on the table around Mr. Carramba.

"Here is your sandwich," said a teacher, handing a paper bag to Bramwell Wink-Porter. "It is bologna and shredded carrots with extra mayonnaise, the favorite lunch of the Fuzzy Bunny in your wonderful book."

"I did not write that book, you know," said Bramwell Wink-Porter.

"I am Mrs. Wheatbeet," said the teacher. "I have written a book, too. It is called *Bunnies in Love.* I have it here. It is nine hundred pages long. I wonder if you would read it while you eat your lunch."

"It is a very long book," Bramwell Wink-Porter said.

"If you like, you can give me your address," Mrs. Wheatbeet said. "I will bring you the book, and I will wait in my car while you read it."

"Perhaps that would be better," Bramwell Wink-Porter said.

Bramwell Wink-Porter tried to eat his sandwich. It was a large sandwich, and slippery. A slice of bologna squirted out of the sandwich, and stuck to his shirt.

Another teacher sat down. "I am Mrs. Heatseat. I think it is wrong that animals do not wear clothes. I know you agree with me, because the Fuzzy Bunny always wears a raincoat."

"Well, you know, I did not write that book," Bramwell Wink-Porter said, with his mouth full.

"I would like you to sign this petition," Mrs. Heatseat said. "When we have enough names we will send it to the President, so he will know that many people want animals to wear clothes."

Bramwell Wink-Porter signed the petition. He got mayonnaise on the paper.

"It is time to visit the fourth and fifth grades," Mrs. Feenbogen said.

"I have not finished my sandwich," Bramwell Wink-Porter said.

"We have to hurry," Mrs. Feenbogen said. "Don't forget your bunny hat with ears."

The fourth and fifth graders were waiting in the gym. "The children have a surprise for you," Mrs. Feenbogen said.

The surprise was drawings. The fourth and fifth graders had drawn large pictures of the Fuzzy Bunny on sheets of paper, with colored chalks. They gave their drawings to Bramwell Wink-Porter. Soon his arms were full of Fuzzy Bunny drawings. The colored chalk got all over his clothes.

The fourth grade had brought their mascot. It was a large bunny. "Please pet our bunny," the fourth graders said. The bunny bit Bramwell Wink-Porter on the thumb.

"Yaaaay!" the fourth and fifth graders shouted.

"I will take Mr. Bramwell Wink-Porter to Howard the janitor to have his thumb bandaged," Mrs. Feenbogen said. "Say good-bye to Mr. Wink-Porter."

"Good-bye, Mr. Wink-Porter!" the fourth and fifth grades shouted together.

Mrs. Feenbogen took Bramwell Wink-Porter to Howard's room in the basement. Mr. Carramba was sitting in a chair, holding a bag of ice to the back of his neck. When he saw Bramwell Wink-Porter's thumb, he said "Oooh!" Then he slid from the chair and fell to the floor.

"He has fainted again," Howard the janitor said. "I will take care of him later."

Howard the janitor bandaged Bramwell Wink-Porter's thumb.

"It is time to visit the sixth grade," Mrs. Feenbogen said.

"Let's go," Bramwell Wink-Porter said.

"You are a brave man," Mrs. Feenbogen said.

The sixth graders were waiting in the library. "Hey, Doofus!" one of the sixth graders shouted. "You've got a slice of bologna stuck to your shirt, and there is colored chalk all over your clothes!"

"We will be quiet," Mrs. Feenbogen said. "And listen to what Bramwell Wink-Porter, the famous author, has to say."

"Good afternoon, boys and girls," Bramwell Wink-Porter said. "I would like to tell you a little about the work and life of an author."

"Do you know any famous people?" a sixth grader shouted.

"Do you know any basketball players?"

"Do you know Michael Jordan?"

"No. I do not have that pleasure," Bramwell Wink-Porter said.

"Do you know Bart Simpson?"

"Isn't Bart Simpson a cartoon?" Bramwell Wink-Porter asked.

"You look like a cartoon yourself!" someone shouted.

"Mr. Wink-Porter!" a sixth grader asked. "Remember in *The Fuzzy Bunny* where the Evil Weasel catches the Fuzzy Bunny?"

"The fact is, I did not write that book," Bramwell Wink-Porter said.

"And remember where the Evil Weasel ties the Fuzzy Bunny up?"

"Well, I haven't actually read it, either."

"And the Fuzzy Bunny unties himself by making his muscles vibrate?"

"Well, no, I don't actually – " Bramwell Wink-Porter began.

"Could you show us that?"

"Show you?"

"We have some rope. We could tie you up, and you could escape like the Fuzzy Bunny."

The sixth grade swarmed around Bramwell Wink-Porter, and began to tie him to a chair.

"Children, I am sure Mr. Bramwell Wink-Porter would like to spend more time with you," Mrs. Feenbogen said. "But now it is time for you to return to your classrooms."

"But we haven't finished tying him up!"

"Perhaps Mr. Bramwell Wink-Porter will come back someday, and you can tie him up then. Would that be possible, Mr. Wink-Porter?"

"I would be delighted," Bramwell Wink-Porter said.

The sixth graders left, muttering to themselves.

"Now you have met all the children in our school," Mrs. Feenbogen said. "It was very kind of you to visit us."

"Thank you," Bramwell Wink-Porter said. "I enjoyed my visit."

"Now I will escort you to your car," Mrs. Feenbogen said.

In the hall, they met a second grader, wearing a Fuzzy Bunny mask and hat. "Mr. Wink-Porter," the second grader said. "I have one last question to ask you."

"What is your question?" Bramwell Wink-Porter asked.

The second grader asked, "Do you think you might ever write a book about us?"